I am Edison

I am Edison

David Webster

With illustrations by Sophie Jonas-hill

Matador
Unit E2 Airfield Business Park,
Harrison Road, Market Harborough,
Leicestershire. LE16 7UL
Tel: 0116 2792299
Email: books@troubador.co.uk
Web: www.troubador.co.uk/matador
Twitter: @matadorbooks

ISBN 978 1803134 918

British Library Cataloguing in Publication Data.
A catalogue record for this book is available from the British Library.

Printed and bound in Great Britain by 4edge Limited
Typeset in 14pt Minion Pro by Troubador Publishing Ltd, Leicester, UK

Matador is an imprint of Troubador Publishing Ltd

For Matt, Maksim, Vinnie,
Meliah, Leya, Sophia and Leonardo.

"Come, my beloved, let's go on an adventure together."

Chapter One

The Eternal Forest

—~—

Edison was lost, very lost, more lost than he had ever been.

The problem with moving into a new area as a family is that you don't know where you're going and you rely on Mum and Dad to be your guides, your anchor and your roadmap for finding your way around, especially when you are walking in a forest.

He had only stopped for a minute to examine what he thought was something military, a piece of metal, maybe left over from the Second World War. (He was really interested in the War; his great-granddad had been in it and he'd watched a box set about it on the television.) It was part of a tube sticking out of the ground with writing on it. It had that green army paint look and felt a bit dangerous. He hadn't touched it – he knew not to do that – but he had stopped to make out the writing and in that time the rest of the family, who were already ahead by some metres, continued to walk on out of sight.

Now, when he looked around, he couldn't see them anywhere and what's more he wasn't really sure which track they had gone off on. So, he tried one of the tracks, not really worried at this point and confident he would catch them up quickly. It was then that all the trees began to look the same and there was no beaten track to follow. It seemed as if the trees had moved around deliberately to confuse him and catch him off guard. *No, that would be nonsense*, his mind told him, although his feelings said something else.

That's when he began to wander, trying to guess his way out of the woods. Surely, he wouldn't have to go far to get back on track and rejoin the rest of the family. He tried shouting, "Mum, Dad, where are you?" He tried several times, but there was no reply. The reality that he was lost began to dawn on him. He began to feel a bit anxious as he continued to search the forest with his eyes – he was more and more convinced the trees moved when he wasn't looking at them. Fortunately, he remembered what his dad had always taught him to do when he was worried. Stand still, take a deep breath and decide what to do next before you move off again. So that's what he did. It took a few seconds but soon he knew what to do.

Of course! Keep going in a straight line and he was bound to come out somewhere, a path, a road maybe, something that would lead somewhere. Or so he hoped. For several minutes he tried this but came across no new paths or tracks. He was just beginning to doubt the wisdom of his action when he suddenly found himself in a clearing. It was maybe twenty metres by twenty metres, enough to let more light in and give him the feeling of being somewhere welcoming and friendly.

Until then, most of the trees in the wood had been the tall spindly type, silver birch and others he couldn't name. Here in the clearing there was a huge oak tree; its trunk was nearly two metres thick and its upper branches outstretched the surrounding trees. He noticed how the bark on the tree curved upwards as if someone had twisted the whole tree half a turn. For some reason Edison found the oak comforting and reassuring, as if the tree gave off an air of wisdom and knowing.

"Who dares stand in the shadow of the Great Oak?" a deep voice bellowed out.

As the vibrations of the voice struck Edison's ears, he realised that the oak tree had grown a mouth, a chin, a nose and two eyes with bushy brows. What had seemed like two lower branches became arms with spindly fingers, one of which gestured in his direction as the tree spoke.

"I said, who stands in the shadow of the Great Oak?" the oak repeated.

"Err, my name is Edison," he replied. He had seen this kind of thing before but only in cartoons and *Lord of the Rings* movies.

"What kind of name is Edison?" the oak tree said less loudly.

It was a question, but it felt like an accusation you might get from a bully in the playground or from a teacher who didn't like you.

"It's a good name; my parents gave it to me," he said, feeling like this was a moment to defend his name, not just back down. This was only a tree, after all, albeit a talking one. *It probably can't move – can it?*

"No, I mean, what kind of name is it? What does it stand for? What does it mean?" the Oak said, sounding friendlier.

Edison felt reassured and continued. "Well," – *Am I really talking to a tree?* he thought – "I think I am named after Thomas Edison, but mainly my parents just liked the name."

"Just liked the name. Mmmmh!" sighed the Oak, and carried on speaking like he had just looked up the name in a name dictionary or googled it. "In old English, Edison comes from the name Eadwig; Edison is the son of Eadwig. The name Eadwig has two parts, 'Ead' and 'wig'. 'Ead' means 'prosperity and fortune' and 'wig' means 'war'."

"Really?" said Edison, a bit bemused.

"You could say 'prosperous and warlike'!"

"Oh, I see," said Edison, although he didn't really, this being his first experience of talking to a tree anyway.

"What do you believe about yourself?" the Great Oak continued.

"Believe about myself?" said Edison, trying not to appear confused.

"Yes, what do you believe about yourself? Who do you believe you are?"

Edison stopped to think. Before now he hadn't believed in talking trees. Now he was being asked what he believed about himself. *If this is a dream, please can I wake up*, he thought.

Just at that moment he remembered something else his dad had taught him; it just popped into his head. *When you don't know how to answer a question, ask a question back.* He had never imagined where he would need this bit of advice, but this seemed as good a time as any.

"What do you mean, what do I believe about myself?"

The Great Oak continued speaking a little more slowly in order to make his questioning as clear as possible. "What do you believe about yourself? Who do you believe you are? A simple question! Two simple questions, in fact."

It didn't seem simple to Edison. What was going on here? He was puzzled, and when he got puzzled, he got frustrated, and when he got frustrated, he got annoyed. Was this just a dream? *It must be a dream*, he decided, *no matter how real it feels.*

"Where am I?" he blurted out, a bit angrily.

"You are in the Eternal Forest," the Great Oak said calmly, waving his spindly arms in an open fashion to indicate the forest around them.

"The Eternal Forest?" Edison replied, still puzzled and none the wiser.

"Yes," the tree answered without any further explanation.

The Great Oak paused while Edison thought about this. Then another question came to Edison.

"Do all of the trees in the Eternal Forest talk?" he said with a questioning look on his face.

"No, just a favoured few like myself. Although they all listen," the Great Oak replied, lifting one hand up and cupping it to his ear.

"Listen?" Edison asked. "Listen to who?"

"Why, the Great One, of course. He is always speaking. You will hear him if you are prepared to listen."

"Who is the Great One?" Edison ventured, the puzzled look growing on his face. This was beginning to feel like one of those discussions in the school classroom when your mind wanders for a minute or two and then when you come back into it you are not sure what people are talking about.

"Mmmmhh!" the Great Oak mused. "Why, the Great One is mighty and powerful, awesome and terrifying, and his voice is like flashes of lightning that shakes the desert and twists trees," he added grandly.

As the Great Oak spoke, he waved his arms around enthusiastically and then when he said 'twists trees' his voice slowed and he first looked down and then slowly up to indicate to Edison, if he hadn't noticed already, the way that the bark on his trunk twisted round. Edison wasn't an expert on trees, but he wasn't sure he had ever seen an oak whose bark twisted like that of the Great Oak. He was impressed but continued with his questions.

"He sounds a bit scary to me?" he said, taking a half a step backward.

"Scary! Scary! Of course, he is scary," the Great Oak replied loudly, looking straight at Edison and leaning towards him whilst narrowing his eyes, which made his bushy eyebrows stand out in an imposing manner. Then, relaxing backward and with a softer, more lilting tone of voice, he said, "The Great One can be scary, but he is also merciful and kind." As he said this the surrounding trees seemed to sigh and gently sway in agreement.

"There, you see, they are listening, just as I said before." The Great Oak folded his arms with satisfaction at having his point demonstrated so clearly.

A few minutes ago, Edison hadn't talked to a tree, or a Great One, whoever they may be. But he was intrigued.

"Would the Great One speak to me?" he asked.

"Of course, if you will listen," replied the Great Oak, once again leaning towards him and looking him in the eye.

"What kind of things does he speak about?" continued Edison.

"Just about everything, really. Just about everything," the Great Oak repeated wistfully. Then, while resting his right elbow on his left hand and pointing towards Edison with his right finger, he said, in a wise and friendly voice, "He particularly likes names. Yes, he does love a good name." The Great Oak paused and then added, "He loves naming things and letting others name things too, for that matter. His names always mean something. Yes, he is very strong on naming and names."

As he spoke this time his eyes had begun to wander and look into the distance, but then they suddenly returned to look directly at Edison.

"Do you have any other names?" he said, turning slightly and leaning forward so as to look at Edison with one bushy eyebrow raised.

"Yes, I do, as a matter of fact," he managed to reply, wondering where the conversation was going now.

"Good, good, well done, well done," the Great Oak said, patting the air with his right hand as if he was patting Edison on the head for doing something well.

Then, with a happy sound in his voice, he concluded, "Well, that's my job done. Enjoy the rest of your walk. Oh, and remember, don't forget my previous question, 'Who do you believe you are?' Goodbye!"

And with that the Great Oak's mouth, chin, nose, eyes and bushy eyebrows just disappeared and his arms returned to looking like branches should look like again. In fact, the Great Oak, which had at first seemed to stand out from the other trees, now just melted into the background of other oaks just as large and significant as itself. Soon it became impossible, from Edison's point of view, to pick the Great Oak out from the rest.

Edison stood still for a few moments not knowing what to think. *Why did the Great Oak rush off like that? Did he have another appointment? A bit more explanation would have helped. All that stuff about names and the Great One was all very interesting, but it doesn't get me out of this forest. A few directions might have helped.* He could feel himself getting annoyed inside. *Why didn't I ask him to at least point me on the right track? I am still lost, maybe even more lost. How do you get out of this place, what's it called, the Eternal Forest? What was that silly question as well? Who do you believe you are? What kind of question is that?*

However, Edison knew that some of his best thinking came after the event, especially unusual ones like this. So, he sat down on a nearby log, still annoyed but keen to figure it all out if he could. He picked up a nearby stick and began to draw in the bare, dry soil at his feet. It seemed to help him control his growing sense of fear, as the loneliness of his situation returned to him. The idea that this was an Eternal Forest didn't help much. *What does that mean? It goes on forever? A never-ending forest? How do you get out of that?* In his annoyance he threw the stick into the forest. It hit a tree, making a banging sound, and then the forest remained silent. He decided he'd better give it some more thought before he moved on. As he did this, the Great Oak's question came into the forefront of his mind.

"Who do you believe you are?"

He'd never thought about that before. "Who do you believe you are?" *I am Edison*, he said in his head. Then out loud he said his full name. "I am Edison, Maksim, Nathaniel Vincent," pronouncing the 't' at the end of Vincent with more force. *That's my name, that's who I am*, he thought. *Isn't that enough? I am not someone else; that's who I am.* And with that, because he had no fresh ideas and the Great Oak hadn't given him directions, he decided to head off in as straight a line as possible whether the trees were moving around or not.

If only he had a compass, that would help. But he didn't. Still, give it time, he would come out somewhere, and he wasn't feeling hungry yet, so that was a good thing.

"Who do you believe you are?"

The question kept surfacing in his mind. He certainly wasn't naturally negative about himself like some of his friends seemed to be. He knew when he was worried other worrying thoughts could come up in his brain. He'd been shocked once by a teacher who had called him stupid. It was in PE and he thought he had been doing well up until that point. They had been doing gymnastics and it was his turn to vault the horse. He had run at it confidently at first but then fear had got the better of him halfway down his approach and he'd bottled out of the jump. Rather than slam into the horse he'd decided to just run round it.

"You idiot, Vincent! Don't be so stupid! Do it again and don't bottle out."

Mr Smith the PE teacher was not normally that nasty. He was strict but good-humoured and usually encouraging. Perhaps he was having a bad day. Perhaps he'd had some bad classes before this one. Perhaps his football team wasn't doing well in the Premier League? Perhaps he was getting divorced? Who knows? But for Edison it stung and it stuck. PE with Mr Smith was never the same and he was glad they had another teacher the next year.

If someone says you are an idiot and you are stupid, does that make you an idiot and stupid or are you just not good at PE? He was pretty good at Maths and History, so that counts, doesn't it?

Who is Edison Maksim Nathaniel Vincent?

He is good at Maths and History.

But an idiot in PE?

Where does that leave me? he thought.

He wandered on, puzzled, trying to keep in a straight line. If this was a dream, perhaps he would soon wake up. The crunch of the leaves beneath his feet seemed to suggest it was real enough.

Chapter Two

The Winged Lion

—⚬—

The talking tree had been weird, but he could do with something like that again to help him on his way. It had occurred to him that being in the Eternal Forest was like being in Narnia but without the snow, or the dwarves, for that matter, and of course Aslan the lion and the wicked queen. *Were there four children?* He couldn't remember. His mum and dad had read him the stories when he was younger. *Was there a talking tree or was that another book?* He didn't always get on with his brother and sister, but he wished they were around just at that moment. *Still, at least it wasn't snowing!*

On he trudged. It wasn't getting any clearer. In fact, the trees seemed to be getting closer to one another, making it harder, if anything, to keep in a straight line and feel you were going in the right direction. He wished he had a drone, like his older cousin in Manchester. Then he would soon have a great view from above and discover he was near the edge of the forest and not far from getting back with the family and going home. *This must be one of those days when Mum and Dad made us leave our phones at home so that we spoke to one another and didn't get loads of digital interruptions during the day. Shame. With the satnav I would have been home and dry, back with the family by now.*

Soon the trees were so close together it became almost impossible to know what a straight line was and he noticed that the trees were increasingly blocking out the sunlight, creating a gloomy, slightly forbidding atmosphere around him. He heard a low howl in the distance mixed with a sudden breeze through the upper branches of the trees and the wild flapping of a number of birds who had been disturbed by something. The ground beneath him began to soften and feel squelchy, and he could make out the beginnings of a damp feeling in his trainers. He tried to backtrack to a drier part, but the wet soil was all around him at every turn, it seemed. *How did I suddenly end up with wet all around?* he thought. He tried to get back on track, looking more and more for some dry ground or raised tree roots to place his feet on.

What was that? Something moved. In the corner of his eye, he caught sight of some movement in the trees. What exactly, he couldn't make out. Then the same again on the other side of him. He began to move a little quicker, trying to jump from one dry area to another. This became more and more difficult as small pools of water began to appear and multiply as he edged his way forward, going from tree root to tree root. Once, he nearly slipped and ended up in one of the pools, just reaching out to grab the trunk of a tree in time. As he inclined his face downwards a frightening image stared up at him from a nearby pool.

"Arrgghh!" he exclaimed, as the face of a ghoulish creature rose up to the surface of the water and then disappeared. If he had remained looking down others may have appeared, but he turned away, with the tree he had grabbed firmly to his back. He stared into the forest only to realise the gloom was increasing and more things seemed to be moving among the trees. There was the low growling sound again. He decided the best course of action might be to run for it and take his chances with the pools of water, which he hoped would be quite shallow. So, he launched off from the tree and took several pools in his stride, and sure enough, they were only a few centimetres deep. Despite the fact that he could soon feel his socks getting wet through, he was glad to be on the move and making his escape from whatever troubled that part of the forest. He couldn't have been running and leaping for more than a few seconds, though, when he leapt into another pool which proved to be far more treacherous.

"Ugghh!" he exclaimed as he felt both feet sink into the thick mud below. The momentum of his body thrust him forward as his feet were sucked deeper into the black gunge beneath him.

"Woah!" he cried as he nearly lost his balance going forward and then arching backward and then forward again, until finally he was able to spread his arms and get his balance by bending his knees.

"Oh no! Some kind of bog or quicksand. Just my luck," he said, realising he couldn't raise either of his feet out of the mire below. They were stuck fast and now the water was just below his knees. Looking around there were still things moving between the trees which, try as he might, he could never really identify. Were they humans or animals? He could never quite make out. There was another howl, this time much nearer than before, and then, horror of horrors, the same ghoulish face he had seen earlier loomed even larger in the pool before him.

He cried out again in shock and grabbed one of his legs with both hands in a desperate attempt to free up one of his feet.

"Come on, come on!" he cried, straining with all his might. It would not move. He tried the other.

"Come on, come on, you…" He looked up momentarily to see if the ghoulish face was still there and whether the things in the trees had closed in further and were making themselves known. Instead, a bright light had appeared in the middle distance and was advancing closer and closer towards him. As he peered through the trees, he could see they were moving to one side to form a passageway for something or someone to make their way through. *Is that a hushed sigh they're making and are they bowing?*

Edison's attention was drawn to his feet again because he could feel himself being raised up out of the mud.

"What?" he exclaimed as the legs of his trousers emerged from the water of the pool bone dry.

Looking up quickly to check the advance of the light, he could see it had begun to take on some kind of shape as it continued to progress through the parting trees. Edison could certainly make out legs, not human ones, and eyes, bright sparkling eyes and golden skin, or was it fur? Nearer and nearer, it drew, and further and further his feet were raised up out of the sticky, mirey mud, all clean and dry.

Wings, wings, yes, those must be wings, he said in his head as the brightness drew nearer. Now his feet were completely clear of the mud and his trainers were not only dry but perfectly clean as well. The pool around him dried up and the trees had parted sufficiently to reveal a clearing where the sunlight shone in and the gloom and sense of threat simply disappeared.

Then in the next instant, there, slap bang in front of him, bordered by two magnificent silver birches, was a lion, a lion with wings. *This is Narnia*, he thought, *except Aslan didn't have wings*. The wings made him look taller than he actually was, plus he shone so brightly Edison fell back onto his rear end on the ground. He wasn't sure whether he was going to be eaten or spoken to. Was the Lion a good sign or not?

The Lion gave a low growl, not too threatening but enough to keep Edison transfixed. And then another low growl, slightly louder. He thought about making a run for it but couldn't decide quickly enough. *Where did I throw that stick? Not much defence against a lion.*

The Lion, casting his eyes around the clearing and peering deep into the surrounding trees, let out a loud roar. He breathed out a powerful, extended breath, almost like wind as he paced around the clearing, until he had done a full circle and returned to the spot where he had arrived.

Wherever he went the many pools of murky water dried up and the trees parted again and light streamed back into the forest. As the Lion breathed out his husky roar Edison thought he heard the words, "be clean, be clean" repeated several times, but he couldn't be sure. Anyway,

he was glad the forest was restored to a light and much more friendly place – no more treacherous pools and no more ghoulish faces. He followed the Lion as he progressed in a circle and noticed how noble and majestic he seemed and what power and authority he had over the trees and pools. Whatever the things were moving in the trees they seemed to have gone as well.

He still wasn't sure about the Lion – was he for him or against him? He felt slightly better when the Lion lowered his wings against his body, took a few paces back, smiled and sighed a warm, welcoming sigh. "Hmmmh! Good, very good," the Lion added, appearing to be well pleased with whatever had just happened.

Edison slowly stood up again and took a few slow paces backwards himself just to give a little more escape room if he needed it. To his surprise the Lion then sat back on its haunches with his forelegs still straight and sighed again, continuing to be very pleased with himself. The silence between them continued for another few seconds and Edison began to wish that this lion would talk a bit more, like the one in Narnia. Another thought entered his mind. *Well, if he attacks or eats me, I'll probably wake up. I usually do from a nightmare. Then I can go downstairs and have a drink and biscuits; that's what I am allowed to do with nightmares.* It was a consoling thought but quickly broken by the next sound from the Lion.

"What is your name?" the Lion finally said in a deep tone. As he said it Edison felt the Lion's eyes looking straight at him in a knowing kind of way. It made him feel that if he lied (not that he would) the Lion would know it. He was happy to be honest and truthful, anyway. After all, the Lion was only asking him what his name was.

"Edison. I am Edison," he replied cautiously, still wary of his imposing questioner.

"Ed-dis-son. Ed-dis-son." The Lion spoke with a long, less growly tone, but drawn out and powerful.

Keeping surprisingly calm, he replied, "Yes. Edison, that's me."

"Good, very good," said the Lion, still speaking in a drawn-out way. There was a long pause. Edison wondered if this was really a talking lion, or one who only talked occasionally, or one who did talk a lot but just recently had forgotten how to and was now starting to practise again. His questions were answered when the Lion spoke once more.

"Edison, that's your name. It's a good name, a powerful name."

"I don't know," he said. "I have never really thought about it." He wondered why there was all this talk about his name. Was his name a code to get out of the forest, perhaps? He loved maths and he loved codes. *If I figure this name stuff out, will I be able to find my way out of here? Is this a code-cracking exercise? Is my name the password?* But what the Lion said next took an unexpected turn.

"I am here to give strength to your name."

The way the Lion spoke made it sound as if he knew Edison was coming. *How did he know that? Still, how did you know anything in this place – the Eternal Forest?* He didn't understand so he stuck to his 'asking another question' technique.

"How do you give strength to a name?" Edison asked.

"I breathe on it," replied the Lion as he rose onto all fours and slowly began to circle round Edison.

That sounded a bit disgusting to Edison. He'd always been told not to breathe on things; he could be spreading germs. *In the pandemic everyone had to wear masks so we didn't breathe our germs over other people.* That went on for months, he remembered. On the other hand, he had just seen the Lion breathe on the forest and get rid of all the foul pools and ghoulish faces and those other things that moved in the forest. *His breath can't be all that bad if it can do that*, he thought. Still wary, he decided to circle round himself, keeping his distance from the Lion with enough room to make an escape if he needed to.

"I breathe on people and they get stronger," the Lion continued.

"How do you mean?" Edison eyed him more closely and kept on walking in a circle.

"They get stronger on the inside. They become who they are supposed to be." The Lion spoke with great confidence and authority, as people often do who know what they are talking about.

"Who am I supposed to be?" Edison blurted out, surprising even himself, but partly because all this talk about who you are, or who you are supposed to be, just made him increasingly puzzled.

"That's for you to decide," the Lion said obligingly. "Have you met the Great Oak?"

"Yes, do you know him?" Edison replied, glad to be able to answer a simple question this time. Edison stopped circling at the mention of the Great Oak, as did the Lion.

Although the Lion had asked him the question Edison had the feeling that he already knew about his meeting with the Great Oak.

"He is an old friend, a very dear, old friend. We go back to the beginning."

"I see," said Edison. He didn't really see at all, but he had noticed it was the kind of thing adults say when they partly see and partly don't, when they are not sure but want to appear intelligent.

"Did he ask you what your name meant?" Lion continued.

"Yes, he did. How did you know that?" Edison leant forward, his interest in what the Lion was saying growing.

"Like I said, we go back a long way. Now, what did he tell you your name meant?"

"I think he said Edison was once Eadwig a long time ago. It means 'prosperous and warlike'."

"Did you understand what he was getting at?"

"Not really."

The Lion drew a little closer, just a few metres away from Edison.

Edison knew when people did that kind of thing they had something important to say. He hoped lions were the same. He listened carefully.

"Often parents give names to their children without knowing what they mean. But someone else knows and wants you to know how powerful a name can be if you believe."

Edison felt that sounded mysterious but truthful. He wondered whom the 'someone else' was – but he didn't feel he could ask. It seemed impolite to interrupt.

Again, the Lion leaned forward and spoke reassuringly. "I cannot make you become what your name suggests, prosperous, good in battle, perhaps, but I can strengthen you in your quest to know who you truly are. Would you like that?"

Edison ran out of replies and for a moment took his eyes off the Lion and looked at the ground. It seemed OK to be silent and consider what the Lion had said.

The Lion continued to encourage him, smiled at Edison and looked at him with wise-looking eyes.

"Would you like to be strong inside?"

"I suppose so," he replied, a warm feeling beginning to stir in his heart.

"Would that be helpful to you?" the Lion said kindly.

"Yes, I guess so," he decided. He had begun

to feel the lostness of his lostness and so an offer of help became easier to accept.

Where did he need strength? With certain people at school, certain situations in the playground, with certain teachers? Certainly, in getting on with his brother and sister, even sometimes with his mum and dad. Sometimes he felt anxious for no apparent reason; they were the scariest times. At those times the enemy seemed to be within; the darkness was most dark, like you were in a battle and someone had stolen your sword (that was another dream he used to have). Yes, he decided he needed strengthening. *What's there to lose? What you do in a dream doesn't have to ruin your life, does it?*

The Lion had paused, as if he knew Edison was thinking, but then he continued. "Just lie back and you will feel my power come upon you."

Edison wasn't sure about that at first, but something about the Lion made him trust him. His words were firm and kind, and he felt like the Lion knew him, and this overcame any fear he had. So, he slowly lowered himself to the ground. As soon as his head touched the grass the Lion breathed out and a blanket of warm air flowed over him, starting at his feet, working up his body and then surrounding his head. There was a slight mist surrounding him and Edison could smell something freshly baked. It felt like eating a good meal or drinking a favourite drink.

Then the Lion spoke again, slowly. "Be strong, Edison. Be very strong. Be very strong and courageous, mighty warrior."

With his eyes closed now, Edison lay there, feeling the effect of the Lion's breath and the impact of his powerful words. He felt good, he felt calm and then something very strange began to take place. It began on his head. He could see it in his mind, a helmet resting on his head, the type that Roman soldiers used to wear (Edison recognised them from history websites they had seen in school). Then a breastplate formed around his chest, a belt around his waist and ancient shoes formed on his feet. In his right hand he could feel the weight of a sword, one of those short swords that Roman soldiers would use to jab their enemies at close quarters. On his left arm there was strapped a shield, all polished and shiny on its outer side. With each piece of armour, he first saw it in his mind and then felt it on his body. However, when he ventured to open his eyes, he could see nothing, but the feeling was so powerful he was convinced the armour was there. It made him feel powerful.

While all of this was happening Edison could sense the Lion walking slowly around him, occasionally breathing out again and uttering other words he could just about make out:

"Do not be afraid, just believe."

"It is the Great One's will that you be strong."

"Be strong and courageous, mighty warrior."

Then it all went silent and the feelings in his body passed and Edison sat up. He couldn't tell how long the whole experience had taken. It was like time had stood still for a short while. He wondered whether he should ask the Lion what time it was and how long he had been 'under the influence', of what he didn't quite know? He stood up and brushed his trousers and his hoody, which had some bits of leaf from the forest floor attached to them.

"Arh, there you are," the Lion said in a friendly manner. Edison noticed he was standing at the edge of the clearing as if he was about to depart.

"Now, follow me," the Lion said, and with that he began to walk into the forest.

"Just a minute," Edison called out, still coming round from his experience on the ground.

"Where are you going?" he asked anxiously, worried that he was about to be left on his own, just as much lost as before the Lion appeared.

The Lion turned his head and didn't reply immediately. He looked straight at Edison with his large, all-knowing (and to Edison, all-seeing) eyes and said, "Just follow me, I will put you on the right path." The Lion's voice had a strong note of mystery.

"What is the right path out of here? Can you give me directions then?" Edison replied, suddenly remembering he needed to know how to exit the forest.

"I cannot give you directions, but I can show you the right path." Lion paused and then continued. "They are not necessarily the same thing."

If the Lion had sounded slightly mysterious before, this last comment was definitely even more mysterious to Edison. The Lion walked on a few more steps, but Edison hesitated; he wasn't sure whether to follow the Lion or not.

"Where are we going? What is this all about?" he called out, with a slight hint of pleading in his voice.

He had a strong feeling that he just wanted to be at home, in the warmth and comfort of his mum and dad and the rest of the family, tucked up warm on the settee with a hot meal on his lap and a good movie to watch.

The Lion stopped, turned his head towards Edison and paused before he spoke again. "You must trust me, Edison, if you are to discover who you truly are," the Lion said reassuringly.

Edison didn't really understand what the Lion said, but this sounded like the question the Great Oak had asked him, "Who do you believe you are?", which had puzzled him ever since it had been asked.

"The way ahead may not be easy, but sometimes you have to give up something in order to gain something else – you have to lose some life in order to gain it!" Lion continued.

That sounded like a riddle, and although he loved riddles and codes, he remained puzzled by the Lion's strange words. However, there was something in the way the Lion spoke that reminded him of good teachers that he had had, who loved the subject they taught and probably loved their pupils as well, though they never said so; it just came through in who they were.

"Remember, nothing is impossible for the Great One. Trust him and trust me and you will find your way," the Lion said as he turned his head forward and began to walk on into the forest.

Watching the Lion move on Edison realised it was probably now or never. He had to decide whether to follow the Lion or not. He couldn't really stay in that part of the forest. Perhaps the murky pools, and ghoulish faces, and the things that moved around which he could never quite see would return. 'Trusting the Great One', he didn't know what that meant. Trusting the Lion – well, that was different. Though he could be scary, he seemed kind and he had made him feel strong. He did seem to want to do him good and help him discover who he truly was, although Edison didn't fully understand what that meant either.

"Wait, I am coming. Wait for me," he cried, as he took the first hurried steps in the Lion's direction and followed behind him.

"Good, keep following me – it will be the making of you, I am sure," the Lion said without turning around.

They walked on together for several hundred metres until a well-worn path came into view and the Lion turned to face Edison. Once again Edison was captured by those all-seeing eyes.

"Now, Edison, I must leave you. You must keep on this path. Be watchful and alert, and remember, be strong, be very strong and courageous."

While Edison was still taking these words in the Lion spread his powerful wings and with several beats in the air, he took off up through the trees and was quickly lost to Edison's sight. He had wanted to shout out, plead for him to stay, but something inside prevented him. Despite the Lion's departure he did feel strong inside. Whatever the challenges were that lay ahead he felt ready in some way for them. He felt good inside, like you feel after a meal of your favourite pizza, or after a good day out with the family, or that feeling of victory in the changing room after your team has just won a match. He was certainly less afraid of the forest than he was before and surer of the journey ahead. Perhaps that was the strength the Lion spoke of. He picked up another stick and thrust it this way and that as if he were holding a sword. *Shame it isn't a real sword – it could be useful for hacking through the trees if they moved in on me.*

He now felt much better about the journey, strengthened, ready for anything. He strode off, confidently following the path that the Lion had led him to – into what, he did not know.

Chapter Three

The Winged Ox

—◊—

It wasn't long before his newfound strength was tested.

He continued walking along the path the Lion had led him to. He didn't see any strange movements between the trees, but he wasn't always sure the trees weren't moving around and making things more difficult for him. Then he began to hear something crashing through the forest. It wasn't quiet and it wasn't comforting. It was knocking down trees. Fear returned and he braced himself for the worst. The Lion's footsteps had been soft and measured, but this was a completely different sound. The thunder of hooves was unmistakable. How many and what nature of beast he had no idea. He decided to take cover behind the nearest big tree, hoping his newfound strength would control his fear.

As the beast came nearer, he realised the trees were not so much falling as moving out of the way, as if they were being drawn to one side like in a picture with a wide-angled lens. He felt for the armour that seemed to cover his body, but it didn't seem to be there. *What do I do now? Where's the strength the Lion gave me?* Where there was no clearing before there was now a clearing (similar in size to the one that opened up around the Lion) and in it stood a large winged ox. He chanced a glimpse around the tree at the new arrival. If the Lion had seemed fearsome, this creature was more fearsome still, with huge shoulders and rippling brown muscles. Its wings had all the majesty of angel's wings. Its head was shiny as if it had been anointed with oil. Its breath was deep and powerful, and it had some of that slobber bulls and cows have around their mouths. But it wasn't this that caught Edison's attention – it was his eyes. His eyes were different; they made him different from the rest of his fearsome form. There was kindness in his eyes.

"You can come out now. No need to be afraid," the Ox said in a surprisingly welcoming voice and with a glint in his eye as if he knew exactly which tree Edison was hiding behind.

Edison wasn't bold enough to reply straight away. He thought about legging it away as fast as he could but realised the Ox would soon outrun or outfly him.

"Edison. You are Edison?" the Ox continued. He spoke with a quiet authority as if he knew him.

"Edison, don't be afraid, it is time for us to have a good talk if you are ready?" Ox said kindly, turning aside and taking a few steps around the clearing so his eyes were not on Edison behind the tree.

Edison still wasn't sure, but there was certainly a friendliness in the Ox's voice which appealed to him. Then, without thinking about it, he smiled, and when he smiled a feeling of joy began to rise up inside him, small at first and then growing bigger and bigger until he could not contain it and it burst out in a laugh. He tried to stifle it by putting his hand over his mouth, but another laugh broke out, and then another, and another, and another until he was almost doubled up with laughter. He soon realised that hiding behind the tree was a waste of time and he literally fell out from behind it, unable to retain what was bubbling up inside him.

"Arh, I see the joy has given you strength, or perhaps you just couldn't help yourself, or both," Ox said, breaking out in a bit of laughter himself.

"I, I don't know..." Edison began, and then failed to continue as the laughter took over again.

"The joy has given me what?" he tried again, but again collapsed in laughter.

"The joy you are experiencing is part of your strength," Ox explained before he too continued laughing.

Edison shook his head, not really understanding, and for a few minutes all that he and the Ox did together was laugh and laugh until their bellies ached. (Even the trees seemed to join in quietly.) They laughed at each other laughing, with Edison pointing at the Ox and the Ox pointing back with his hoof. When Ox pointed his hoof at Edison he fell over and rolled about laughing uncontrollably. This went on for several minutes until both the Ox and Edison finally recovered and their conversation continued. Edison was bemused and still a

little giddy from so much laughing but fearless enough now to answer Ox's original question.

"Yes, I am Edison. How do you know my name?" he managed to ask.

"I was sent to find you," Ox replied with the same knowing tone that Edison had heard from the Lion.

"Err! Why?" Edison asked, and, wondering if that was too abrupt, added, "Why were you sent to find me?"

"Because you are lost, of course," Ox replied, raising his head as he said it.

Edison turned his head from side to side. *How do these people, or animals, know these things?* he thought.

"Sent to find me? Who sent you? If you don't mind me asking?" he added politely. Despite all the laughter between them, which Edison still didn't really understand, the Ox was still an awesome-looking creature who he instinctively knew deserved respect.

"The Great One sent me." The Ox seemed to stand taller as he spoke of the Great One.

"The Great One? Who is the Great One?" *The Lion spoke about him but never explained who he was talking about. Am I supposed to know who he is?*

The Ox paused and Edison felt uneasy again. *Have I asked a question I should already know the answer to?* Unease turned to embarrassment, that feeling you get when you have said the wrong thing in class and everyone turns their eyes on you. He tried to cover up his ignorance.

"Oh, do you mean the Great Oak?" That seemed like a good reply, the best he could do in the circumstances.

"No," the Ox replied slowly, "the Great One is not the Great Oak; he is much greater than that."

"So, do you know the Great Oak as well then?" He was a bit surprised at himself for asking this. Perhaps that strength thing was working after all.

"Yes, I do," Ox replied. He paused again but took a step closer to Edison.

Edison wasn't sure where to go next with the conversation. He began to wonder if these animals needed a bit more training on how to deal with twelve-year-old boys who have never done this sort of thing before. He thought of supply teachers in school who don't know their stuff or couldn't control the class.

Fortunately, after some consideration, the Ox continued. "I have stood in the presence of the Great One and have come to give you a gift, Edison, because you are highly favoured," he said with a broad smile on his face.

"Highly favoured? Me, really?" said Edison, feeling increasingly puzzled.

"What kind of gift?" Edison asked.

He couldn't see anything the Ox might be carrying. Was he being honest with him? All those he had met in the Eternal Forest so far had seemed pretty honest. He had no reason to suspect the Ox would be different, had he? Equally, this place was pretty magical so maybe the Ox could just make a gift appear.

"Err! Thank you," was all Edison could think to say.

"You're welcome," the Ox replied.

There was another one of those awkward pauses where Edison didn't know what to say. He put his hands in his pocket and moved one of his feet around in the soil in an aimless kind of way. Another question was in order, perhaps. He took his hands out of his pockets and opened them up towards the Ox.

"Err! Was the gift for now or for later?" He was impressed with how politely that came out.

"Don't you want the Great One's gift now?" the Ox replied.

"Well, of course…" Edison began, clasping his hands together.

The Ox took a step closer, tilting his head backwards as if he were wearing a crown and looking with one kind but penetrating eye deeper into Edison's eyes.

"Do you doubt the Great One's ability to give what he has promised?"

"Not exactly, it's just that…" Edison said hesitantly.

"To create something from nothing? To declare what is not as if it is? To give his gifts to those who will receive?" the Ox continued.

That was complicated and Edison didn't have a reply. The Ox sounded really clever, a bit like his mum and dad and teachers at school.

Edison still didn't know what the gift was but again thought he should know and was apologetic about not knowing and not realising what the Ox, or the Great One, could do. To his relief the Ox spoke again, this time stepping back one step, gently lifting his wings in readiness for some act of kindness.

"You are Edison, are you not?" Ox continued.

"Yes," he said rather meekly (*I thought we had established that*).

"You are Edison the Prosperous, Edison the Warrior?"

"Well, yes, if you say so," he replied hesitantly.

"You are also Maksim, are you not?"

"I am. Who told you that?" Edison said, trying quickly to get across his next question before the Ox replied this time. "Don't tell me; the Great One told you?"

"The Great One knows everything," the Ox said, still holding his head high in a regal fashion. "But on this occasion, it was the Great Oak. He knows all your names and all the meanings of your names."

That's strange, thought Edison. *Didn't the Great Oak ask me what my other names were apart from Edison? If he knew my other names, why did he ask me what they were? Perhaps he knew more than he was letting on. Very mysterious!*

Stepping closer to Edison, Ox looked him in the eye and said, "Do you know the meaning of the name Maksim?"

Edison tried to remember what Maksim meant but couldn't, which annoyed him because he was sure he did know it once. He remembered asking his mother, who always knew the answer to things like that (and of course a great deal more).

"So, remind me," – the question-asking

technique again – "what does the name Maksim mean?"

"It has the same root as the name Maximus, the great Maximus of the Roman Empire and means simply, 'greatness'," he said, still with his head raised in a regal posture.

"Yes, that's it, 'greatness'!" Edison exclaimed (his mum had told him that before).

"That is my gift," said the Ox, lowering the front of his body and legs in a sort of bow.

"Your gift?" Edison felt he should bow too and settled for a nod in the Ox's direction.

"Yes, my gift to you. Strictly speaking, the Great One's gift to you." The Ox's eyes of kindness seemed to grow even kinder as he spoke.

"How can greatness be a gift?" In Edison's mind gifts came on birthdays and at Christmas, all wrapped up with themed paper. He'd had superhero paper in the past but not recently; he thought his parents might think he was growing out of that phase.

"How can it be a gift if you can't see it?" He opened his hands and moved them left and then right as much as to say, "Where is it?"

He was hoping the invisible gift would materialise. These animals could do that sort of thing surely, and anyway, in dreams all things are possible. A Christmas Eve expectation of presents started to grow inside him.

"Trust me," said the Ox kindly. "Greatness is the gift I have come to give you."

"How can I be great? It doesn't just happen like that. And besides, I am only twelve, twelve and a half actually," he said a little indignantly.

"Again, I say, trust me," the Ox replied patiently. "You are Edison, Maksim. You are designed for greatness if you will receive it, if you will believe it."

It struck Edison that he was being asked to do a lot of believing in the Eternal Forest. He still wasn't fully convinced that this was all real. He pinched himself to test whether he was in a dream. It didn't change anything except give him a sharp pain in his side.

"I know you are thinking, *this gift will make no difference.* You may even think this is all a dream."

How do these animals know what I am thinking? Edison thought again.

"But trust me, as you received strength from the Lion you will also receive greatness from me."

The feeling he had received from the Lion suddenly rose up again inside him just as the Ox spoke of it. He felt stronger, ready to do something, though not sure what. Like when you return to school from the summer holidays and you have new teachers and new subjects and you are back with friends and school is interesting again (for a while at least).

"What do you think greatness is?" Ox asked.

Edison found that a rather abstract question. "I am not sure what you mean," he replied.

"Well, who would you call a great person, for instance?"

Edison felt sure he must know some great people, but his mind went blank for a moment before he recovered his thoughts.

"Well, Winston Churchill would be one. There was a king called great... what was his name... *we did him in history*... Alfred, the Great. Yes, him. Oh, and Mrs Pankhurst, who won women the vote," he said, pleased with himself that he was able to recall a range of great people.

"Very good," Ox replied.

While Ox paused again some other names came into Edison's mind, but these were mainly celebrities from the TV and sport and reality programmes. They were well known, but he doubted they were great, so he didn't mention them.

"So, do you think you could be great like that?" Ox enquired.

Edison thought hard for a moment.

"Not really," he said quietly, glancing down at the ground as unwelcomed thoughts began to cloud his mind. Where did they come from? Why, suddenly, now? They were far from great.

The time I kicked the neighbour's cat. I know I shouldn't have done it, but it came every day and sat next to our pond, and I was convinced it had taken some of our fish.

When Jack (a friend) had dared me to steal sweets from our local shop. Called me a coward if I didn't. He'd done it and it was easy, so why didn't I? Worst still, I got away with it. Never did it again. Slipped a pound coin under their door when they were closed to cover the cost of the sweets. Still felt guilty about it, though.

Lied to my parents once and still haven't told them it was me who broke the glass vase. Fortunately, a window was open next to it and they accepted it was the wind that blew it over. Whew!

Often argue with my brother and sister – doesn't everyone? They usually start it – well, perhaps I do as well, occasionally. Well, more than occasionally.

"I know what you are thinking." Ox's kind voice interrupted his train of thought. For some reason Edison didn't doubt that Ox knew what he was thinking and that made him feel even more guilty and ashamed of his thoughts.

"You can be great, but not as most people understand greatness. Greatness can come to the least of people, whatever their past and whoever they think they are," Ox said wisely. He had a way of gently nodding his head and then raising it in the air when he was saying something important.

"Come with me for one moment," the Ox said as he walked over to the right-hand side of the clearing with Edison dutifully following him. As they did so the trees parted and a magnificent scene opened up before them. Edison recognised it instantly as a medieval banquet, the kind he had seen in his history books and on information boards on school trips to castles. There was a large table set out furthest away from them, the top table, no doubt, where the Lord and Lady sat, or perhaps it was a king and queen. Other nobles sat with them on either side and then many other important-looking people sat at two long tables set at right angles to the top table, ending quite near to where Ox and Edison stood. Everyone was finely dressed and an abundant amount of food and wine was already presented on the tables. There were minstrels to one side playing their instruments enthusiastically and loudly so as to be heard above the talking and laughter from the assembled crowd. There were also a small army of servants, men, women, young and old serving those who were seated. Some ferried in yet more food, some were serving guests wine, others were slicing meat and they created a constant stream going back and forth across the room.

For a while the Ox just looked and chuckled at the scene and Edison noticed he was tapping one of his hooves to the music. After a while he turned to Edison and said, "Let me ask you a question. At this banquet who are the great people?" Ox asked, turning his head so Edison caught the twinkle in his eye.

Edison could spot a trick question when he saw one coming and this was certainly one of those. He scratched his head (partly playing for time), but he couldn't work it out.

"The nobles, the king and queen, I suppose," he answered, although he doubted what he thought was the obvious answer was the right one.

"I am sure that is what most people would say. But greatness resides with those who serve, so the great people are the servants," Ox replied.

"But the servants could be anyone," Edison objected.

"My point exactly," replied the Ox, doing that raising-his-head thing he did again. "We can all serve others, and that is the doorway to greatness."

"So, are you saying if I am going to be great, I need to become a servant or a waiter?" said Edison, crossing his arms and not feeling enamoured about a future career waiting on tables.

"Serving can take many forms. It's not a career; it's a life. It's the way you do things, loving others, forgiving people, giving to those in need, listening, doing to others as you would hope they would do to you," Ox replied.

Edison vaguely remembered that last phrase from somewhere. *Was it in RE or did Mum and Dad say something like it? Whatever!*

Edison wasn't feeling great after remembering some of the bad things he had done in his life. The list of serving ideas seemed pretty hard to him too. This was just getting worse. The effect of the laughter was well and truly worn off by now and he wasn't feeling great inside at all. Perhaps it was time to draw things to a close – surely the Ox wouldn't mind if he made an excuse to leave?

"I was just wondering," – always a good way to introduce an excuse – "I was just wondering, if you didn't mind, I will be getting back home now. Homework to do, you know, that kind of thing. Parents might be worrying about me. They don't need to, of course, but you know what parents are like."

Ox just sighed slightly and seemed to ignore his excuses. "It's time to press on, Edison. Trust me. There will be a time for returning home at the journey's end."

At that moment Edison had half expected to be walking back into the forest the way he had come, but Ox ploughed on with his next question regardless. "Are you ready to trust me? Do you want to receive your greatness?"

"Well, yes, I think so, but I don't feel very great just at this moment," he said honestly.

"That's the thing, yes, that's the thing. You don't have to be great to receive greatness," Ox exclaimed, taking a step towards Edison to underline his point. "That's why it is a gift!" Ox said, again holding his head high as he said it. "It's something you are before you become it.

Like when an acorn becomes a great oak tree –
ask the Great Oak – it starts small. All that the
great tree becomes later, when it is fully grown,
is contained in the small acorn," he said firmly,
as if to conclude a winning argument.

"I see," said Edison. He didn't know if he was
agreeing with him or just humouring Ox so he
could get going towards home.

"Do I have to lie down?" Edison said,
remembering his experience with the Lion.

"No, not unless you want to." The Ox tilted
his head in a reassuring way.

"I'd rather stand if you don't mind."

"No problem."

And with that the Ox simply spoke loudly
and boldly into the air. "Arise, Edison Maksim.
Receive the greatness you are called to. Arise
and shine. Walk into your greatness."

At the word 'walk' Edison felt himself step
forward a few steps. He didn't know why; it
seemed the right thing to do, the sort of thing
great people do, perhaps. Was he great now? He
didn't know. How would he know?

"You will know," the Ox reassured him with
both a smile and his eyes of kindness.

*There it is again! These animals, people,
persons, whatever they are, seem to be able to*

read my thoughts. Are they mind readers or what? But they are kind with it.

Now more questions he wanted to ask the Ox started to flood into his mind. But before he had a chance to ask any of them the Ox beat his wings several times and took to the air, repeating several times, "You will know. You will know. Just be watchful. Be watchful. Be alert. You will know."

Soon he had disappeared over the treetops.

You will know. You will know? I don't really know what I am supposed to know, or to believe, for that matter. They expect you to do a lot of believing in this place. Be watchful? Be watchful about what? Strange things in the trees, those again? Who knows?

Edison thought about these words. He didn't really understand belief and believing. He didn't pay too much attention in RE lessons and just did enough to get by. His family, especially his mum and dad, believed a lot of things and read loads of books about faith and healing and that kind of stuff. He had grown up around churches, people singing songs and hymns, but most of the time he took these things for granted.

You will know, the comment kept repeating in his mind.

He was inclined to believe what the Ox had said. *After all, it worked with the Lion and they seemed to be on good terms, even friends. Animals, even weird animals, could be, I suppose.*

He decided to walk on. As he did, he strode along not with lots of questions this time but with what seemed a new confidence. Thoughts of returning home slipped to the back of his mind.

Was it the strength, was it the greatness or was it the strength of greatness?

He was pleased with himself for putting the two together in his thinking. Even the trees seemed to open up a bit more as he walked along, and his path seemed straighter and straighter. It suddenly struck him that the Ox had given him no help with directions. He, for his part, had been so caught up with and sometimes confused by their conversation he had forgotten to ask him.

Ox had said something about a journey, about finishing a journey. That was the closest he came to it. Well, I suppose I have no choice but to follow the straightest route possible and hope it comes out somewhere.

Was he beginning to trust more? He certainly felt better inside. For no apparent reason he recalled the laughing episode with the Ox, and as soon as he did, he began to laugh again, not uncontrollably but enough to make him feel good inside and a bit stronger than he otherwise might have been.

Do I even feel great? he thought.

The pathway he was on grew brighter and the trees around him seemed to be friendlier as their top branches swayed gently in the breeze.

Chapter Four

The Angel

—⚡—

As Edison walked along the land began to slope downwards, gently at first and then getting steeper and steeper. It wasn't long before he came across a stream that was cutting through the land and creating the slope. As he descended it became harder and harder to keep his straight line. Then he realised that a stream would probably become a river at some point and the river would certainly lead him to buildings and to people and eventually to his family or someone who could tell him where he was and how to find them. He decided to follow it.

The further he went down the valley created by the stream the deeper and wider the stream became. The sound of rushing water grew louder and louder too. Eventually he found himself clambering over bigger and bigger rocks as he made his way down. The stream, which was really now a river, became a series of cascading torrents and small waterfalls and got wider and wider. Edison paused on one of the higher boulders and looked ahead where the river became a series of wild rapids. It reminded him of the white-water experience he and his family had had on holiday in Wales last year. He began to wish that he had a boat he could launch into this river; how brilliant that would be!

While he was enjoying this thought, he felt a sudden gust of wind on his back. Before he could turn to see where it was coming from, the slight wind became a powerful force and he heard the familiar sound of a beating wing. Instantly, he was propelled off the rock and down into the rapids below. He only fell a few metres and the current was strong enough to prevent him hitting the riverbed. However, his whole body knew he was in deep trouble as he tumbled along in the rapids, gasping for air and trying to keep his head above water. His arms and legs flapped around as he fought desperately for air and for something to grab that might get him out of the torrent. In his panic, his breath came in sharp gulps and he feared he might be about to drown. One of his feet then got caught in a cleft between two rocks and he felt the pull on his body as it jerked to a halt below the water. The current was forcing him downstream, but his foot was held fast between the rocks. He felt a horrible wrenching feeling around his knee as one of his ligaments tore under the pressure. He let out a scream of pain and terror, but his mouth just filled with water. All he could see was white water cascading around him. He felt he was going to die. The force of the water tilted his body violently, back and forth. But then one particularly strong gush of water threw his body so violently one way that it twisted him free, even though he felt as if his foot had been severed at the ankle in the process. He was free and speeding downstream still, gasping for breath and trying to stay above the lashing waves.

The torrent bumped him along for the next fifty metres, when a large shadow came over him and he felt large hands grab him firmly under his chest and miraculously lift him up out of the water. He breathed desperately but freely again and looked down on the waters below, their menacing beauty no longer a threat. He closed his eyes in exhausted relief. Whatever or whoever had hold of him brought a feeling of peace which only increased as he was set down on a large rock a little further downstream in the warmth of the sun. But peaceful relief was immediately interrupted by searing pain from his ankle and leg and a multitude of other bumps and bruises which now demanded his attention.

"Arrrrggggggghhhhh!"

His cry of pain was long and deep. It was total agony, for what seemed forever. He was out of the danger of the water but now he thought he might die of the pain. Through his tears he could see a large shadowy figure, presumably the thing that had rescued him. It was approaching. Edison was horrified again because for the first time he remembered the wind and the beating of wings that had led to his falling into the rapids in the first place. He was overwhelmed with fear and helplessness; tears blurred his eyes and he didn't really see what happened next. He felt a hand touch his foot and another hand touch his knee. A voice said something, but he couldn't make it out. An intense warm feeling filled his foot and his leg and then moved rapidly through the rest of his body. The storm of pain ceased and he felt surrounded by something, enclosed and protected. He could barely see because of his tears and kept his eyes closed most of this time, only occasionally trying to peer through the watery haze. Little by little a healthy, alive feeling returned to his body. His crying stopped and he breathed a deep sigh of relief. To his amazement he felt completely normal.

"Are you all right?" he heard a voice say.

"Yes, I think so," he replied, looking around in the direction of the voice.

He rubbed his eyes and got a clearer view of where the voice was coming from. It was a figure, a human figure, a woman. She wore a checked shirt, jeans and trainers, and her blonde hair was tied back in a bow. She had large shining angel wings which grew out of her back and rose up sharply towards the sky. All in all she stood three to four metres above him. He sat up to get a better look at his rescuer.

"You have had quite an ordeal," she said, crouching down again more to his level. She spoke with a soft, reassuring voice, like his mother, Edison thought, at her most comforting.

"Yes, I suppose I have," he replied. He knew his words didn't really convey how close he thought he had come to dying.

Again, he recalled the wind and the beat of wings and the shadow. He was going to ask the angel about them but wasn't thinking clearly enough to do that and something told him not to at that moment. Instead, he said, "Who are you?" He got to ask his question first this time.

"I am Mattea," she said as she sat on a nearby rock just above him.

"Are you an angel?" He felt silly asking, but he wanted to be sure.

"Yes, I am an angel," she replied in a straightforward manner.

"Oh. Well, thank you for rescuing me." He felt good remembering the politeness his parents had drummed into him over the years. He stood up and felt the awkwardness of his wet clothes.

"What was that thing you did with your hands?"

"The thing that made you well?" she said, holding the palm of her hand up towards him for a second or two.

"Yes." He felt his leg and ankle to just check they were still better.

"That was your healing."

"A miracle, you mean?"

"Yes, a miracle; you would call it that in your world. It's normal where I come from."

"Where do you come from?" he said, looking around for the first time at the place in the river his tumbling had taken him to.

"I live with the Great One."

"Don't tell me he sent you to me." Edison was beginning to get the pattern of these appearances; they had a lot in common.

"You are right. He did send me." Mattea nodded her head and crossed her arms.

"Is it something to do with my name?"

"Yes, it is."

He felt encouraged by getting these things right; like getting two or three answers right in class (which rarely happened to Edison) it gave him a warm glow inside. He also realised that he had begun to feel hungry before but didn't now. Had the angel's hands fixed that as well? He pressed on, hoping to get a few more things right.

"Is this to do with my third name, Nathaniel?" he asked brightly.

"Yes, correct. You learn quickly." She waved an approving finger at him.

The angel had a way of saying things that made you feel good, as if she really meant it. She asked the next question.

"Do you know what Nathaniel means?"

Mattea leant forward slightly and her right eye half closed and looked at him more intently.

He had had a good run of right answers, but it finished there.

"No, I am sorry, I don't." He looked around nervously, hiding his ignorance. He noticed how the river calmed down at this point and began to flow more smoothly beyond the torrent.

"Don't worry, it's not a test. Nathaniel means 'gift of God'."

He was surprised that he had never considered the meaning of his third name. *The ones in the middle do get a bit neglected*, he thought. A question then popped into his head. "And what does your name mean?"

"Mattea? 'Gift of God' also," she said, smiling to acknowledge the shared meaning of both of their names.

"The same. Wow!" He opened his shoulders in surprise and stepped back on one foot. "Never thought of myself as a gift. What does it mean?"

"What do you think it means?" she said with a twinkle in her eye. She reminded him of his mum and the way that adults get you to think things through for yourself.

"I don't know. My parents have sometimes said I am a gift from God."

"That's right, you are," she said, now with a broad smile on her face.

"I thought they were just being nice, you know, like parents are." For the first time he found himself smiling at her.

"They probably were, but do you think they really believed it?" she asked him.

"I guess they did. My mum and dad do believe a lot of things."

"Well, there you are," Mattea added with a gesture of her right hand towards him.

"Yeah! A lot of things now I come to think of it." He stopped to think of some of the things his parents believed that he had taken for granted a lot of the time, like saying 'please' and 'thank you', being good and praying to God. Yes, they believed in a lot of things.

"They believe in lots of things, but I can't remember many at the moment."

"And today. Was today a gift?" she said, continuing her inviting smile.

"Well, falling into the rapids wasn't much of a gift, was it? I nearly died." Some of the hurt of what had just happened to him returned and he felt his leg again to check it was really OK.

Mattea placed her hands together and continued to speak wisely and kindly. "Perhaps that is hard to see, but was what happened next a gift?" Her hands still together, she gestured towards him.

"Oh! Yes! Definitely. It was definitely a gift. You saved my life. You healed me." This time he ran his hands across his chest to check that his healing was real. The bigness of what had just happened to him seemed to overwhelm him and he fought back his tears again.

Mattea stepped forward and placed her hand on his shoulder to comfort him. "So, do you think getting your life back helps you to see what a gift you have and what a gift you are?"

"I guess so, yes," he said, looking up into her eyes and feeling the warmth of her smile. He felt puzzled and didn't understand the difference between having a gift and being a gift. But being a gift felt good.

"Well, in that case my work here is done." She withdrew her hand and stepped back a few steps.

"Oh, are you going now too? No one stays long enough; they always leave."

"Yes, we all leave." She paused but then added, "For the time being at least."

"So, I take it you are friends with the Great Oak and the Lion?" Edison said cleverly.

"And the Winged Ox too," Mattea added before he could go on.

"Let me guess, you all go back to—"

"The beginning," Mattea said, finishing his sentence.

They both laughed several times and Edison had to try hard to restrain himself from laughing too much, joy welling up inside him as he recalled the laughing fit he'd had with the Ox.

Mattea restored the conversation. "Just think about what each of us has left you with. What has each creature, the Lion, the Ox and I, Mattea, left you?"

"Oh, I see, yes. Well, the Lion gave me strength, the Ox gave me greatness and you… you…" He tried to put it into words, but Mattea did instead.

"I have helped you to see that you are a gift from God."

She opened her arms and held out her hands to him.

"Now stretch out your hands and take hold of mine," she said.

As Edison did this, he felt a strange warmth flow from her hands into his and then into the rest of his body.

"Edison, Maksim, Nathaniel, you are a gift from God," Mattea said. The tone of her voice was so much like the Lion's and the Ox's, Edison thought, firm and loving at the same time.

For a few moments all Edison could think about was the warm glow flowing through his body. It felt just like the healing he had received a few moments ago.

"I am a gift from God," he said, looking first at his arms and hands and then up into Mattea's face, which appeared radiant and so, so kind.

"You are Edison, the strong."

"You are Maksim, the great."

"You are Nathaniel, gift of God."

With each declaration from Mattea Edison felt a fresh wave of warmth flow through his body.

"Strength, greatness, gift of God," Edison said several times over, hoping this would help him remember it.

As he said this Mattea moved a few steps away from him and spread her wings. "I must leave you now. Continue on your journey."

"Do you have to go?" Edison asked, again feeling disappointed at her sudden departure.

"I am afraid I must," Mattea said, giving no further explanation. "Remember, give freely from what you have received," she said, taking a step back.

"Yes, I will," replied Edison, not fully sure what she meant. "Which way do I go? Do you have any directions?" *At last, I get to ask someone that question.*

"Just follow the river, just follow the river," she replied reassuringly. "Be on your guard and be watchful on the rest of your journey," she added, with a note of concern.

This sounded just like the last words of the Lion and the Ox, but before he could ask what he needed to guard against or be watchful about Mattea had flapped her wings and taken to the sky, ascending rapidly over the surrounding trees. Within a few seconds she was out of sight.

He sat down among the rocks at the river's edge with a mixture of wellbeing and disappointment at being left on his own again. He was still trying to take this meeting with the Angel in when it dawned on him again that he was still lost. *I suppose I should be thankful for one clear direction. I wonder where the river leads?* He was really grateful for all the Great Oak, Lion, Ox and Mattea had said and done for him, but he also longed to be home. The day was getting on and he still hadn't found his family. But strangely, he wasn't hungry now.

Looking down the river, he realised the next stretch that he could see was beyond the rapids where the river calmed down and began to wind more slowly and the land opened into a plain. A well-worn track he hadn't noticed before opened up alongside the river. The sun was still catching the rippling waters and seemed to welcome him to follow the river's course. *This must be used by others, so buildings and people can't be far away*, he thought.

He set off confidently down the path beside the riverbank.

Chapter Five

The Temptation

—⁓—

Edison wandered along the bank of the river for what seemed a long time. The bank was lined with trees and he longed for a rope to swing out over the river. His family had done this on holiday once where the campsite ran down to a similar river where you could swim in the water. For the first time he began to feel really tired and he was also hungry again. He wished he'd packed an apple or a Crunch bar to eat along the way. He wished he was with his family again and his mum was announcing the contents of a picnic tea down by the river. He also realised the sun was fading and the shadows of the trees were lengthening. He was having to take more care about where he placed his feet as the path began to darken.

As he rounded a small bend in the river, he came across a huge weeping willow tree right on the riverbank. Half its branches were draped over the land and the other half over the river. Its yellow colours made it stand out from the other trees and it seemed to invite you to sit in its shade. Edison decided it was time for a rest even though he was concerned that evening was coming on. As he sat down, he heard a noise coming from within the tree. It wasn't a voice (not yet at least), more like a soft rasping sound, the kind a fine sandpaper might make rubbing on a smooth surface. Then something spoke.

"Good evening." The voice was friendly and inviting.

"Good evening," Edison replied, startled. *Another talking tree*, he thought.

"Are you lost?" the voice continued, sounding like a concerned adult helping a child who had got separated from their parents in a crowded space like a railway station or an airport.

"Yes, I am actually," he said, peering into the tree's branches, trying to make out where the voice was coming from.

"Hmm," the voice mused, "that will not do. How can I help you?"

Well, thought Edison, *this voice or tree sounds friendly enough, and this is the first one to offer me help out of being lost.*

"Can you give me directions out of here? I was walking with my family and the next moment I looked up and they were gone."

"I see," the friendly voice continued. "How long have you been lost?"

"Oh, a few hours by now." He realised he had lost track of time amidst all his encounters with the different creatures.

"And have you met anyone else on your travels?" the voice asked casually.

"Yes, I have." He was eager to tell someone about all the things that had happened to him, as if he had returned home and wanted to tell his family of his adventures.

"And did they help you?" the voice enquired.

"In a way, yes." He tried to peer more into the tree and spot where the voice was coming from but could see nothing but leaves and branches.

"Did they give you anything to help you through the forest?"

"Yes, they did," he said, surprised again by the knowledge that these trees and creatures had about things that had happened to him.

As trees go, this one was easy to talk to. He looked for a mouth or nose or eyebrows, like with the Great Oak, but this tree barely moved and had no facial features he could make out.

"What did they give you, may I ask?" The voice seemed a little less casual this time but still friendly.

Edison paused for a moment, wondering if he should be talking to a stranger but decided there wasn't too much risk, and besides, he was still keen to share his story. *The Great Oak said there were other talking trees, and from the outside at least this one looks and sounds friendly.*

"Well, strength, err... greatness and, oh, this Angel healed me and called me a 'gift from God," he said with a little pride.

At the mention of these things, the tree seemed to shiver for a second or two and more than several leaves were loosened and fell to the ground. Before Edison could wonder too much about this the voice spoke again, in much the same friendly tone as before.

"Ahh! You have met the Winged Lion and Winged Ox and an Angel. Let me guess, was it Mattea?"

"Yes, it was! Do you know them all?" Edison bounced a few times on the balls of his feet, excited that this was someone who knew all those who had tried to help him so far.

"Well, of course! In the Eternal Forest we all know one another. We go right back to the beginning."

Edison was sure the willow swayed slightly from left to right and then right to left as the voice spoke in a slower, rhythmic fashion. The tree's movement played tricks with his eyes and he found it quite mesmerising.

"Great, so would you please give me directions to get out of here?" he said a bit impatiently, recovering himself and blinking several times to refocus his eyes.

"Of course, I will. In fact, in a very short time you will be home and tucked up in bed, I am sure. But before you go, I have some gifts for you too."

"Oh, well, I see. Thank you." Much as he was curious about what the tree might have in store, he mostly wanted to get home. He moved about from foot to foot, hoping to accelerate the conversation and be on his way.

"Are they to do with my names?" he asked.

"Your names? Your names?" For the first time the voice seemed unsure and uncertain.

"Yes. The Great Oak and the other creatures explained my names and their meanings, except my last name, which is Vincent, which I know means 'victorious' or 'conqueror.'" (His granddad, who knew a lot about names, had told him that.)

As soon as Edison uttered the words 'victorious or conqueror', the willow shook much more violently than before. Every leaf shivered, as if someone had managed to shake the very trunk of the tree. The whole tree shimmered brightly as the underside of the leaves caught the evening light. More leaves fell to the ground and a low, painful moan could be heard from within the branches as if someone had been stabbed by something sharp. Edison began to think that there might be someone inside the branches and that this wasn't simply a talking tree. He might have ventured inside the confines of the willow, except the violent shaking put him off.

As if recovering from something, a bit out of breath, the voice spoke again. "No matter. I am sure your names are very good, very powerful, in fact. Please let me strengthen you further and perhaps increase your greatness and your gifts – and show you the way home, of course." The voice had recovered its composure.

The mention of home helped him be less impatient. Perhaps a few more minutes wouldn't make any difference.

"Well, I suppose if I can be home in the next few minutes," – that's what he thought the tree meant – "then a few more minutes won't hurt. What did you have in mind?"

"Let me show you." And with this the lower branches of the weeping willow parted, first in one part and then another and then in a third place. In each place there was a small, rectangular box-shaped stand and on each stand, there stood an item. A finger-shaped bulge appeared in the tree, just above the first box, on which stood a small dark brown bottle, the kind medicines come in.

The voice spoke again. "This is a powerful potion; it will give you great strength. You will be able to lift large weights and overcome any bullies at school. You will be invincible! You are Edison, after all, great in battle. This will make you so, so, sssoo strong."

Edison was sure he detected a slight hiss in the way the voice said the last two words. But he ignored it. He was too fascinated by the promise of the potion. Perhaps this was what the Winged Lion really meant by him receiving strength. Strength in his body, not just in his mind. Physical strength would be much more useful in the playground. He pictured one bully at school in particular that he would look forward to putting in their place.

The finger shape in the branches moved over to the middle box, on which there was placed a scroll with a red ribbon and a red seal to hold it in place. The word 'greatness' appeared several times on the ribbon in white letters and the seal had some writing on it, which he couldn't make out.

The voice spoke again. "Edison, Maksim, you are called to be successful in battle and do great things. You are called to greatness. This certificate will guarantee your success in any of your endeavours, any test or exam. It is sealed by the Great One himself."

Edison was sure he heard that slight hiss again, but the mention of the Great One, spoken of by the other creatures, was enough for him to overlook this. If it was real, a certificate like that would be really useful. He thought of all the tests he had done in school and the many others he would do in the future, all the hours of revision he might avoid as well. It was a very tempting idea.

Before he could give it more thought the finger moved sideways to rest above the third item. On this box was a large picnic hamper like the one they had at home. This time as the voice spoke again the lid of the hamper opened, revealing all his favourite snacks and meals. There was his favourite pasta bake, lasagne, spaghetti, breadsticks and baked beans, his favourite main meals. Then there were desserts galore but especially huge doughnuts with all three of his favourite fillings, custard, chocolate and jam (the fillings oozing out of each of them). In an instant his mouth began to water at the sight of this feast.

"Edison, Maksim, Nathaniel, Vincent. Here is your final gift. This gift will feed you whatever you desire, whenever you desire it. You will be able to feed yourself and as many others as you desire to help. With this fast food you will conquer all; you will be victorious."

The last word, 'victorious', sounded as if the voice had gulped halfway through, as if the word had been difficult to get out. However, the sight of food overruled any worries Edison might have had about the voice's pronunciation. He suddenly had an intense feeling of hunger come over him, the kind of feeling that drives you to raid the biscuit tin or push your way through to the front of the queue for school dinners. Only his strong sense of politeness (drummed into him by his parents) and some uncertainty about the nature of the voice stopped him immediately reaching out and grabbing what he wanted from the hamper.

The voice continued, speaking more slowly and purposefully than before. "Please come and partake of the potion of strength, grasp the scroll of greatness, and taste the delights of victory and success."

Edison felt himself sway forward slightly and he almost lost his footing. There was that mesmerising feeling again; he shook his head, steadied his feet and refocussed his eyes on the swaying willow tree. He also noticed the voice stumble over the word 'victory' but ignored it because his hunger was getting the better of him.

He asked a question instead. "Well, I am sure the potion is very powerful and the scroll would be really useful. But I think I will just have the food for now, if it is all right with you? Thank you." His parents would be proud of his politeness, he was sure.

However, he hadn't reckoned on the reaction of the voice or the tree at this moment. It shook violently and more leaves fell to the ground, making the pile around the tree even thicker. He thought he saw something move among the branches again.

The voice spoke once more. "Well, I would love to accommodate you in this, but unfortunately all the gifts go together; you can't have one and not the others or else they don't work for you." The voice sounded a bit harsh and more like a telling-off than an instruction.

"Oh, I see," replied Edison, although he didn't really. His eyes were firmly fixed on the doughnuts now and his mouth continued to water.

"Yes, each releases the power of the other; that's how it works. It's the Great One's secret and I know the others would agree," insisted the voice.

Edison assumed the voice meant the other creatures, but he was too distracted by the hunger to ask. His hunger now seemed to get more and more intense as he thought about the food in the hamper. He couldn't take his eyes off the feast; it seemed to draw him in like a bee towards its honey, like a lion to its prey. He could almost dive in among the doughnuts. What harm could it do? He was the next to speak.

"Well, I suppose just one drop of the potion wouldn't hurt. Do I just have to pick up the scroll? No harm in that. And can I eat as much food as I like? Please!" Even in intense hunger his politeness remained.

"Of course," said the voice, "just a little of the potion will do fine; just hold the scroll, no problem. Just eat as much as you like and your eyes will be open and you will be great, 'successsssful' and victorious." The hiss on successful was unmistakable this time.

He was too desperately hungry to care now whether he got to be stronger, greater and victorious. Fine if it happened but just in this instant all that mattered was that he was hungry. He stepped up to the bottle, unscrewed the top and took a small sip. He grasped the scroll and put it under his arm, and then he dived into the hamper and filled his mouth with doughnuts.

If he had been facing the tree, he would have seen more leaves fall from the weeping willow and be strewn on the ground, even more thickly now, just like leaves in autumn. He would also have seen that the fallen leaves revealed the origin of the voice, a large python-sized serpent, that quickly slithered down from his resting place on a branch and began to circle the ravenous Edison with his huge coils.

"Eat, Edison, eat, my son. Eat as much as you like." The Serpent's words slithered out in the same way that his oily body moved.

When he saw the enormous Serpent Edison's first instinct was to get up and run, but he found he could not. He was inexplicably stuck to the ground and still felt compelled to go on eating the large doughnuts he grasped in each hand. His words came out garbled, muffled as they were by his doughnut-stuffed mouth.

"Who are you? And I am not your son!" he said, struggling to get his words out through the doughnuts that filled his cheeks. He was annoyed and fearful at the same time and there was panic in his voice.

"Oh, but you are mine now, Edison, strong in battle. You are mine, Maksim the great. You are mine, Nathaniel, gift of God. You are mine, Vincent the victorious. You are mine!" As he spoke each name the Serpent seemed to coil himself around the helpless Edison more and more. Edison heard the full hiss in the voice now and he felt a tightening grip on his body as the coils of the serpent began to press in around his legs and his middle. None of the other animals had gripped like this. He could barely move and if not for the Serpent's coils he would have fallen over. He was trapped and like a rising tide the snake's coils kept curling around him and advancing up his body.

He cried out in desperation, "Who are you? Let me go!"

"Why, I am the Serpent, of course. Isn't that obvious?" The Serpent's head was fully visible to Edison now and it reared up in front of him, face to face, its two evil-looking eyes set high in its forehead.

"It wasn't obvious until a second ago! You tricked me." Edison had abandoned his doughnuts and beat down on the Serpent's body with his sticky hands, his blows making little impact on the reptile's scaly skin.

"Of course, that is what I do." As he spoke the Serpent's fangs became visible to Edison, which only added to his terror.

He half screamed his next cry. "You liar!" he said, beginning to try to struggle free. But he was held fast.

"That is true. I have been from the very beginning," the Serpent said with a knowing grin.

"Let me go. I am Edison the great, the victorious. You can't do this to me."

The Serpent only tightened his grip, his coils extending fully up to Edison's chest so that he had to raise his arms in a desperate attempt to keep them free. The sky darkened and the air cooled and the river turned a murky brown colour.

The Serpent spoke this time with an air of authority and menace, as if it owned its newfound captive. "But as you can see, I can do this and more. Oh, and don't worry. You can still be great and glorious and gifted as long as you remain with me, my child, my son," it hissed.

"Look, I am not your child and I am not your son. I already have a family." Edison tried to reason with the creature, but his words felt helpless and useless against the Serpent's strength.

"When you drank the potion, took up the scroll and ate the food, you forfeited your other family ties. You will be great with me. You will be victorious with me. You will rule with me in my Kingdom forever."

The Serpent's coils were nearly up to Edison's neck and he began to fear he might suffocate if they went any higher. The cold feel of its scales and the constriction on his body made him feel sick. He felt his ribs move and breathing was nearly impossible under the pressure of the coils and for the second time in hours he felt close to dying.

"Help! Help! Help!" he cried in a weak voice, but the words came out strangled as he began to suffocate. Tears welled up in his eyes as he made a final cry for help. "Lion! Ox! Angel! Angel Mattea!" *Yes, surely, they can rescue me.*

"Hush, hush, my child. They cannot hear you. I will not harm you. You are mine," the Serpent continued, slightly loosening his grip so as not to kill him.

"I am not yours! I am not yours! Let me go!" The only movement Edison had was from his elbows to his hands now but still he tried to batter the Serpent's body, hoping some of the Lion's strength would come to his arms.

"Go? No need to go. You are home now. You have all you need, all that your names declare. This is where you belong."

"I don't, I don't, I don't!" Edison cried, still struggling, his voice becoming more of that of a small, desperate child than a young boy.

"Come, come, you will get used to it. We have a beautiful forest to explore and I have many other friends for you to meet."

He didn't want to imagine who the Serpent's friends might be. Now the coils were forcing his forearms into the air and his body was losing almost all ability to move. He cried out desperately again, "Lion, Ox, Angel, help me! Where are you?" Edison craned his neck and tried to project his voice.

"Peace, peace, my child. You don't need them, I will—"

Before the Serpent could finish its sentence there was a loud beating of wings, a crashing through of branches and a large shadow was cast over Edison and the Serpent. The Serpent let out a terrifying cry, similar to the one Edison had heard when it was hidden from him in the tree, but much, much louder. Immediately, he felt the grip of the Serpent loosen and he was almost free until, as he stumbled to one side, the tail of the Serpent gripped his ankle and held him tight. The Serpent also turned his body and looked with horror at his attacker – it was the Winged Ox.

Chapter Six

The Battle for Edison

—⁓—

Edison could now see what had caused the Serpent's cry. The Ox had driven one of his horns into its thick flesh and that had caused the Serpent to release his grip on him. The Ox stood powerful and strong on all four legs with half of the Serpent at his feet below his wounding horn and the other half flailing in the air above it. Only the tail of the Serpent was still wrapped around Edison's ankle; he was almost free. Then, to his horror, rather than giving up, the Serpent quickly began to wrap the upper half of his powerful scales around the main body of the Ox and the lower half around his front two legs. This quickly caused the Ox to topple over and at the same time resulted in releasing Edison from the Serpent's hold.

"How dare you challenge my might!" the Serpent threatened, its head now parallel with the Ox's eye as he lay captured on the ground. "You pathetic beast!" it cried, partly in triumph, partly in pain. Then it seemed to suck its body off the injuring horn and seal its own wound.

"How dare you challenge my greatness? You will pay for this insolence." There was a visible tightening of the Serpent's coils and the Ox let out a cry of pain but managed to speak.

"Run, Edison, get away!" the Ox shouted.

"Silence, you fool! He is mine now," the Serpent cried.

"Not for much longer," the Ox said, forcing out each word as the Serpent's coils restricted his breath.

"I won't leave you!" Edison called out, looking around for a weapon of some sort to beat the Serpent – a stick, perhaps – but none was to be found.

"You must go. I have come to take your place." Edison caught a familiar look of kindness in the Ox's eyes.

"What do you mean, take my place?" Edison

said, sitting helpless in the dust, struggling to understand what was going on.

"I must die in your place," Ox insisted, defying the deadly grip of the Serpent.

"No, don't die. Fight back," Edison said desperately, tears once again filling his eyes.

"I must die so that you can go free. It is the Great One's will. You will see later." The Ox closed his eyes and fought for breath.

"No. Fight back." That's all he could say. He had nearly died, now his rescuer was close to dying; he couldn't take it in. Sadness and darkness overwhelmed him. Why was this all happening? Tears filled his eyes.

"Don't cry," the Ox gasped, "all will be well. You will see!"

"Enough, beast. Your time has come. Ha! Where is your Great One now?" the Serpent bit out mockingly. "Free the boy? Why, you can't even free yourself!" he taunted.

Even if he could have fought back, resistance from the Ox was now useless. Every one of his limbs was now bound and unable to move because of the Serpent's deadly embrace. There was then a sickening cracking of bones as the Serpent continued to tighten its grip. The death of the Ox began to seem inevitable.

"All will be well, Edison, all will be well," Ox repeated softly, barely able to get his words out so breathless was he now.

"No! No! No!" Edison cried out in despair.

"Silence, fool!" the Serpent shouted, rearing his head around towards Edison.

"Where is your strength now?"

"Where is your greatness?"

"Where is your victory, oh, gift of God?" The Serpent laughed wickedly.

His laughter shook the surrounding trees and everywhere seemed to darken as evening was hastened on. The whole of the Serpent's body tensed once more to deliver the last vice-like grip that finally broke the Ox's mighty frame. The cracking of bones echoed amongst the trees.

"It is done," Ox gasped, and breathed his last.

"Now, boy, see your saviour die," the Serpent crowed triumphantly, constricting his coils one last deadly time. "So much for your names, so much for their meanings, so much for your greatness!" he spat out with a penetrating hiss.

That was the last thing Edison heard as the Serpent's head reared in his direction, struck him on the side of the head and sent him flying. He scraped his face badly as he hit the ground and then he blacked out.

After a few more moments of the Serpent's tightening coils, the Ox's body became completely still and his spirit gave up the fight. It seemed more like surrender by the Ox than success by the Serpent. Darkness came over the forest and silence was all around.

While Edison lay unconscious the Serpent silently dragged the Ox's limp body and crumpled wings towards the river. With one final heave it cast the dead hulk into a watery grave. Soon, the body was being carried downstream between rocks and boulders, hidden from view by the darkness of the river's depths.

Back on the shore the Serpent began to make good its victory over the small boy before it. Edison remained still and unconscious. As the Serpent slithered along the dusty ground its movement wasn't the same as before the battle with the Ox. The wound from the horn had closed up but wasn't healed, and it made the Serpent's progress uneven and disjointed. Nonetheless, it proclaimed its triumph as it moved to take ownership of its prize.

"Come, little man, now you are mine. Where is your rescuer now?" it said victoriously.

As the Serpent spoke the evening finally progressed into night and the darkness was poorly lit by a distant, shadowy moon. Neither the Serpent nor Edison moved. For a few moments there was only silence.

Faintly, way in the distance, another beat of wings could be heard and coming round at that same moment Edison stirred and turned his head in the direction of the sound.

The Serpent heard nothing but only began to gloat in his triumph. "How easy it was to tempt you with my gifts. How easily you fell into my hands," he laughed.

The Serpent's voice brought Edison fully awake with eyes wide open and he despaired to see the venomous creature still there. His heart sank and his eyes cast around for any sight of the Ox, but there was none. His head fell forwards and he wept with despair. Deep inside he felt sick, lonely, lost and full of regret.

The Lion, the Ox, Mattea, they had all in their own way warned me to be alert, to be on my guard. How could I be so stupid? It was so obviously a trap. Why didn't I see it? I feel bad, very bad. I just want to go home.

A slight breeze passed across his face. The same breeze made the weeping willow rustle; it was not a natural wind. Unaware of this, the Serpent reared up with his head several metres in the air and spoke, "You are mine now. True greatness comes from serving me. True success is being my child." With these words the Serpent declared his victory. Edison lay motionless, fear numbing every part of his body.

Suddenly, in an instant, the breeze that Edison had felt turned to a powerful blast of air blowing through the willow, shaking off more of its leaves. The Serpent turned in the direction the wind was coming from only to be confronted by a pair of large talons that instantly grasped its body in a vice-like grip. The Serpent's scream was only matched by the screech of a gigantic eagle. It descended swiftly and decisively on its quarry, the Serpent unable do more than thrash about wildly, helpless in its failing attempts to loosen the giant bird's paralysing hold. The eagle lifted the Serpent clear of the willow, which finally shed all its remaining leaves. The strong beat of the eagle's wings filled the air with hope as it headed off with its captured prey. The venomous cries of the Serpent grew quieter and quieter as the eagle flew off towards a green hill in the distance.

Edison was alone and deserted again.

He tried to take in what had just happened. Where was the Serpent? Where was the Ox?

Who was this giant eagle? Though relieved to be on his own, he was fearful of the returning Serpent, mournful about the loss of his friend the Ox and still as lost as ever. His body ached from the bruising he had received from the Serpent. He wept again, not as a child but more of a manly weeping.

His tears were interrupted by the beating of wings again and soon the eagle had returned. He didn't know whether to be glad or scared so disturbing had been the events of the evening. Despite the late hour the eagle's presence brought a strange, defused light. It closed its wings, stretched its head up in noble fashion and leaned forward to address an exhausted and puzzled Edison.

"You are Edison, I believe," said the Eagle. It spoke in a warm, firm sort of way, how you might expect a king or queen to speak. Edison attempted, despite his aches and pains, to stand upright, as you would in the presence of royalty.

"That's right. Everyone seems to know who I am. Who are you?"

"I am John!" he said with a regal tone to his voice.

"John? That's a funny name for an eagle," he ventured, not wishing to sound disrespectful.

"Yes, but as you can imagine I am not just any eagle, I am John, the Eagle!" He leant forward as if inviting Edison to take a closer look.

"Yes, I see," he said. He felt so tired and not really ready for a long, complicated conversation. A huge eagle ('the Eagle', indeed) stood before him that was awesome enough. Who was he to argue with that? He was still reeling from his last animal encounter and he had a mixture of guilt and hurt inside him. Then he realised fully for the first time that the Serpent was no longer there.

"Where is the Serpent?" he said, looking round.

"I overcame it and took it away," Eagle said with a note of authority.

"Took it away?" He couldn't quite believe it.

"Yes, somewhere safe. You don't need to worry about it. Well, not for a while at least."

"Is it still dangerous?" Edison said anxiously.

"In a manner of speaking. It is wounded but not dead," Eagle said with a convincing air of wisdom.

"Oh." Suddenly Edison remembered the Ox. "And what about the Ox? Where is he? They were fighting. I was knocked over. I don't remember anything after that."

"The Ox died, rescuing you. The Serpent killed him and threw him in the river," Eagle replied in a plain, measured but sympathetic way.

Edison put his hands either side of his head as if to contain the shock and finality of this news. A heavy feeling of sadness came over him. He wanted the Ox not to be dead. He wanted to hear his voice again.

"I'll never see him again, will I?" Edison hung his head with grief.

"Don't be so sure. Don't be troubled. The Eternal Forest has many secrets no one can fathom."

Edison perked up a bit at this mysterious news but nevertheless he remained puzzled and confused and just stood there, quiet for a moment. Another question surfaced in his mind. "He said he had to take my place. Is that true?" Edison took a step towards the Eagle, wanting to draw out an answer from him.

"Yes, it is," Eagle said, raising his wings slightly from his body.

"Why did he have to take my place?"

"There was no other way for you to be free and forgiven," Eagle replied, as if it should be obvious why the Ox had died.

"Free? Forgiven for what?" Edison looked around as if looking for an answer to his own question.

"Why, forgiven for accepting the Serpent's gifts, of course," Eagle said wisely.

"But they seemed so good and I was so hungry." *Was that fair? I meant no harm by it.*

"They are good and you were hungry. But the Serpent would have made you its slave. It would have taken your greatness and led you to use it for the wrong things. It would have led you away from the Great One." The Eagle raised his voice as he spoke these words as if to press the importance of them upon Edison.

"The Great One. Everyone talks about the Great One. Who is he, or she?" Edison wasn't proud of the way this came out, but he was tired and longed to go home.

"The Great One is the way," Eagle continued.

"The way? The way to what?" He tried to understand what the Eagle was getting at.

"He is your way and my way; he is the way for everyone to find who they truly are."

Those words hung in the air for a moment, and despite his tiredness Edison felt they gave him strength. His mind began to clear. Then he had another question to ask. "What does your name mean? What does John mean?"

John smiled. "It means 'God is gracious.'"

"What does 'gracious' mean?"

"It is from the word 'grace', and grace is love that is given to those who don't deserve it. John means 'God is gracious to me.'" The Eagle tilted his head and Edison saw one of his eyes more clearly. It had the same look of kindness he had seen in the Ox's eyes.

John let Edison think about that for a moment. The night sky grew brighter as stars began to shine and provide added light to that of the Eagle's.

"The Ox took your place. He died in your place, even when you didn't deserve it. That was grace towards you," John added. This time Edison could almost feel the wisdom in John's eyes.

However, he couldn't take this all in. Why did he feel guilty? Why did he give in to the Serpent's temptations so easily? Why had the Ox given his life for him and why did he feel so lost still? *Well, I am still lost, that's for sure.* A fresh wave of tiredness came over him and he struggled to keep his eyes open.

"Would you like me to take you home?" John asked.

"Yes, please," Edison said, raising his head and smiling. That he could understand, and he was relieved to have something so easy to agree with.

John readied himself to fly and turned his back to Edison but then paused, turned his head towards him and asked him a final question. "Just one more thing before I do. Your last name, Vincent, do you know what it means?"

"Yes, I have always known that one, my granddad taught me – it means victory." The thought of his granddad always gave him a warm feeling inside.

"Well, have you just experienced a victory, a great victory?" There was a nobility in the Eagle's voice.

"Yes, I believe I have," he said, scratching his head. As he lowered his hand he added, "I really have!"

Edison's face broke out in a big smile and he felt a great joy welling up inside of him (if he wasn't so tired, he might even have laughed, a good laugh, just as the Ox had taught him). He caught John's eye and there was great joy in his face too as he smiled at Edison.

"Climb up on my back and I will carry you home," John said, lowering himself so that it was easier for Edison to do so. Tired as he was, Edison managed to do as John requested. Gently he placed his arms around the Eagle's neck, nestling himself firmly among his feathers.

Soon, they were both soaring above the forest. Edison closed his eyes and a wave of exhaustion came over him; he felt so very tired. It wasn't long before he was fast asleep under the shadow of the Eagle's wings.

Chapter Seven

I am Edison

—⚭—

As Edison yawned and rubbed his eyes, he wondered where he was and which day of the week it could be. It must be the morning. He was in his own bed, in his own bedroom. Had the Eagle dropped him off at his home? How would he have got his wings through their front door? Had he been dreaming? If he had, why had it seemed so real? As he rose and opened his bedroom door, he half expected to walk into the Eternal Forest, like the children who passed through the wardrobe into Narnia, but he didn't. He was really back home. He decided to go downstairs. He was truly hungry now. That was still the same as it had been every breakfast time since he could remember.

In the kitchen, his mother and father were there getting breakfast for the family. His younger brother and sister had already eaten, and when he arrived, they dashed off to watch something on television, arguing over who was getting to choose what to watch.

His parents had pyjamas and dressing gowns on. He realised it was Saturday morning and no one in the family was rushing anywhere.

"Morning, Edison," his dad chimed.

"Morning," he replied sleepily, pulling out his chair.

"Morning, Edison. Good sleep?" his mum added, kissing his head.

"Yes, very good, although a lot of things happened to me," he said, sitting in his chair and taking his place at the table.

"Interesting dream, was it?" his dad asked, in an attempt to find out what Edison meant.

"Yes, extremely interesting. The most real dream I have ever had." *Can a dream be real?* he thought to himself. It seemed real enough.

"Do you want to tell us about it over breakfast?" his mum said gently.

"Yes, I do," he said. "Yes, I do, I really do."

He didn't know why he said it like that, but he had that feeling of wanting to tell them of an exciting adventure and he thought his parents might be able to explain what the dream meant. They were good at things like that. So, over some toast and jam (quite a lot of toast and his favourite apple and blackcurrant jam) he told them what had happened to him as best he could. His encounters with the Great Oak, the Lion, the Ox, Mattea the Angel and John the Eagle, and how each had revealed something about his names. These parts he could relate with enthusiasm and excitement, but his voice grew quieter as he recalled the Serpent, his gifts and the trap he so easily fell into. He felt sad again when he told them about the Ox's death and he realised that not only did he have a tear in his eye but his parents were moved as well.

"Seems like the Ox knew more than he could tell you at the time," Dad interjected when Edison paused to wipe a tear away.

"Yes, perhaps you are right," Edison replied, and went on to finish the story.

After twenty to twenty-five minutes, he had been able to recall all the main details, which his parents followed with great interest (along with drinking several cups of coffee).

When he had finished, his dad leant backwards slightly, breathed in and said, "Well,

we did choose your names and we did know what they meant at the time."

"Yes, well, do you think I will become those things? Will I be strong? Will I be great? Will I be victorious?"

"What do you think?" his dad asked as he put down his coffee cup.

There, Edison thought. *Dad's using the same question-asking technique he taught me and which was so useful with the creatures in the Eternal Forest.*

"Well, in the dream I felt stronger and braver, especially after all that laughing with the Ox," Edison recalled with a huge smile on his face.

"Well, joy can be a kind of strength, for sure," his mum said. "How do you feel now?" she asked (his mum was good on questions too).

"I feel good. Yes, I feel good. I guess I will know the next time I have to deal with a problem or a challenge."

"That's right," his dad continued. "Knowing the meaning of your names is just a start; believing you can be those things is the next step. They are sort of like a platform you can launch off from for the next stage in your life."

His dad paused to have another sip of his coffee, and then continued, "You are Edison, which means?"

"Prosperous and warlike," Edison replied.

"Maksim?"

"Greatness."

"Nathaniel?"

"Gift of God."

"Vincent?"

"Victorious."

"Yes!" Edison added triumphantly with a fist pump in the air. "Four right answers in a row, not bad," he added.

"You start with believing, then you understand a bit more and then that will help carry you through the challenges ahead," his dad said, smiling.

"I see… sort of," Edison said. He kind of got it, but he didn't at the same time. His parents seemed to have got it, but they were parents, grown-ups, after all.

He thought of another question. "Just because I am named something, doesn't mean I will become that thing. Things don't just happen when you tell them to. Words on their own don't change things, do they?" Edison took a big bit of his toast and let his dad chew on this question.

"Are you sure about that?" his dad continued. "Words can be very powerful, especially when they are spoken by someone who is loving and powerful." His dad looked upwards as if to emphasise his point.

Edison thought about that, and as he did, his mind went back to the Eternal Forest.

"Yes, they all had powerful words, good words," he said in a slightly dreamy but meaningful way.

"All of them, the Lion, the Ox, the Angel, the Eagle – powerful words. Even the Serpent."

A shudder went down his spine as an image of the wily Serpent came into his mind. It jolted his thinking in a different direction.

"I nearly gave it all away, though, when the Serpent tempted me with its gifts. I could have had them all if I had gone its way." He paused to take this in. "I am glad I didn't," he added.

"We all get tempted, Edison," his mum interjected reassuringly. "It makes us feel bad when we give in – guilty, afraid, perhaps a bit lost as well."

"Yes, that's how I felt then – lost." Some of the sadness he experienced momentarily cast a shadow over his mind.

Once he said this, he realised he had felt that way with the Serpent but didn't any longer. Perhaps it was the good feeling of being home, or the warm feeling of several slices of toast and jam in his stomach, or the kindness in his mother's eyes.

"I don't feel that way now, though," he added, a smile appearing on his face.

"Why do you think that is?" *Dad's questions again.*

The image of the dying Ox being strangled by the Serpent's coils came vividly into his mind. "Is it to do with the Ox's death? He said he was sent to die in my place." He knew he was asking a question at the same time as giving part of the answer.

"Does that remind you of anybody?" said his mum, with that same look of kindness in her eyes.

Edison smiled. This story was well known in his household. The One who had given himself for others!

"Yes."

In his heart he knew, perhaps for the first time, the One who had died for him. He truly felt it.

"And how do you feel now? Forgiven?" asked Mum gently.

"Yes, I suppose I do," he said hesitantly at first and then more assuredly. "Yes, I do."

He paused for a moment. He was still anxious about something.

"But what if it was all just a dream? Not real?"

"Dreams can be powerful too," his dad reassured him. "Dreams can be a bit weird sometimes, but dreams have changed people's lives, helped people write songs and books, inspired leaders, even changed nations, so you are in good company," he added.

For some reason Edison felt the side of his face. There was no scrap, but his skin did feel rather rough, and he recalled the blow the Serpent had given him.

Mum's voice returned him to the conversation. "And knowing you are forgiven – that's another good sign," she added.

"Mmmh! Yes, I suppose you are right," Edison said thoughtfully. He had one more question. "Does everyone's name have a meaning? How can they find it out?"

"Well, there are books that explain the meanings of names. Parents often buy them before their children are born or they just look them up on the Internet," his dad answered.

"Or they could ask the Great One what they meant," his mum said, raising her eyebrows and smiling and then taking another sip of coffee.

Edison pointed his index figure upwards and then tilted it quickly once in his mum's direction. "You're right," he said knowingly.

My mum and dad have a way of explaining things that is really good. He smiled at each of them in turn and they smiled back and then at one another.

"So, I can start believing what my names say about me too," he said enthusiastically.

"That's right."

With these words his dad took hold of a wooden spoon from the kitchen table and gently touched Edison on both shoulders. "Arise, Edison the mighty warrior, Maksim the great, Nathaniel gift of God, Vincent the victorious."

Edison stood up and glowed with pride, and then he and his mum and his dad burst out laughing and then all hugged one another for a long time.

As Edison's dad had touched his shoulders and said his names, he knew his father's words had given him that same warm glow he had felt from the Lion's breath and the words of the Ox, Mattea the Angel and the Eagle John. He could feel their words welling up inside him. He took a deep breath – he wanted to mean this with all his heart – as he boldly said,

"I am Edison."

Acknowledgements

—❦—

A huge thank you to all who have helped me write this book: Emily-Jane Hillman for her incredibly helpful editing and encouragement, Sophie Jonas-hill for her inspirational and magical illustrations, and grandsons Maksim and Vinnie for inspiring the original ideas and walking alongside me in the process of writing. Thank you to all the friendly and helpful staff at Matador and finally, to Carol Webster, my most amazing wife – you are my song!

For exclusive discounts on Matador titles,
sign up to our occasional newsletter at
troubador.co.uk/bookshop